Ducks Ducks

Written & Illustrated by Theodocia Swecker

The paintings in this book were done in watercolor
on 140 lb. Arches cold-pressed paper.
The text font is Burbank. Designed by Patrick Turner.

Summary: In the cold of the Nevada mountains, white
ducks help an old mountain lion find a warm spot to sleep.

ISBN 978-1-936097-11-1

Library of Congress Control Number: 2015936728

FIRST EDITION

10 9 8 7 6 5 4 3 2 1

Printed in China

Baobab Press
121 California Avenue
Reno, NV 89509
www.baobabpress.com

BAOBAB PRESS

To my daughter Mackenzie,
who inspired this story,
and to our dog Doc, who now
runs among the stars.

"QUACK, QUACK," said the ducks,
    wishing they had a warm spot to sleep.

"**BURRRR,**" said the old mountain lion.

"I'm tired of being cold."

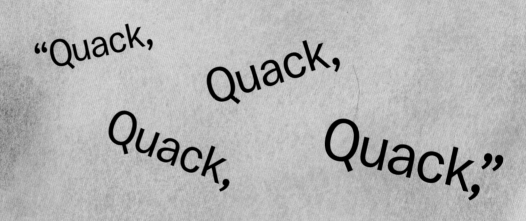

"Quack, Quack, Quack, Quack,"

said the ducks.
"We want to sleep with **YOU!**"

"GRRRRRRR,"
said the old mountain lion.
"I'm going to sleep in my tree."

ᑫᵁ *Quack,* ᑫᵁ *Quack,*
"ᑫᵁ *Quack,*

said the ducks. "We'll go too. We'll join you."

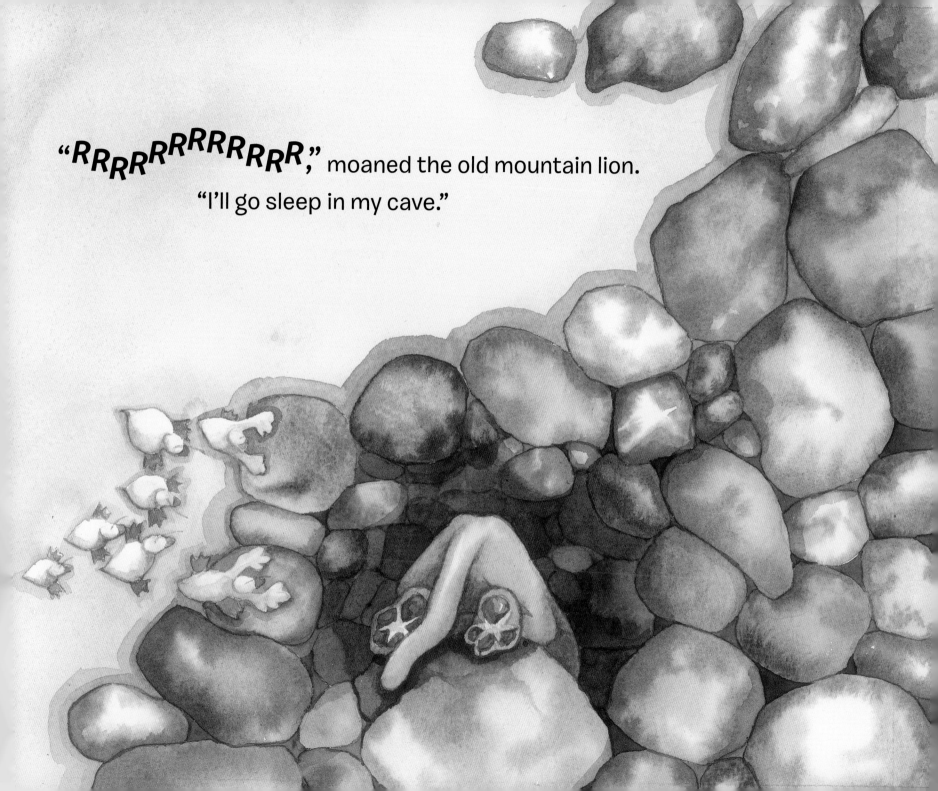

"RRRRRRRRRR," moaned the old mountain lion.
"I'll go sleep in my cave."

"Uggggg," groaned the old mountain lion.

"I'll go sleep on my mountain."

"*Quack, quack, quack,*
quack, quack, quack,"

said the ducks.

"That is an **imPECKable** place."

"**sSShhheeeze**," whined the old mountain lion. "I have no more sleeping spots."

"*Quaaaaaaaack. Quaaaaaaaack.* Come with us," said the ducks.

"QUACK, QUACK, QUACK, QUACK!"

said the ducks. "Sleep here!"

"Quaaaack, quaaaaaack," said the ducks.

A note from the author

When winter comes to Nevada, the wild ducks migrate south and leave behind the Pekin ducks, who are too heavy to fly. These white ducks are sometimes raised by ranchers. In the summer, they watch over households and warn ranchers of impending danger, and in the winter, they swim in the cattle's watering holes to keep the water from freezing. But when they get sleepy and the cold really sets in, they, as well as other native wildlife, must find warm, safe places to bed down.